Oops! I Polluted Again

D0608754

Oops! I Polluted Again

Written by Tisha Hamilton

SCHOLASTIC INC.

New York   Toronto   London   Auckland   Sydney
Mexico City   New Delhi   Hong Kong   Buenos Aires

ISBN 0-439-70003-5

Published by Scholastic Inc.
SCHOLASTIC and associated logos are trademarks and/or registered
trademarks of Scholastic Inc.

12 11 10 9 8 7 6 5 4 3 2   5 6 7 8 9 /0

Printed in the U.S.A.
First printing, October 2005

Oops! I Polluted Again

An Ill Wind

Sapphire Trollzawa stretched luxuriously beneath the aqua satin sheets on her bed. The sun glinting through her window sent rainbows dancing in a kaleidoscopic swirl along the walls and ceiling. Outside, the azure sky was radiant and clear. Sapphire could just tell that today was going to be one of those one-in-a-trollzillion days, the kind of day when even the air seemed to sparkle like a bright crystal.

She bounded out of bed and began getting ready for school. Sapphire's BFFL (her Best Friends For Life) were due to be walking past her house at eight o'clock. As usual, Sapphire would be racing out the door to meet them right on time, and they'd all head off to school together. The five BFFL — Sapphire, Amethyst, Onyx, Ruby, and Topaz — were inseparable. They did almost everything together, including saving Trollzopolis from the evil gremlin, Simon, every so often.

Sapphire hummed a happy tune as she bustled about her bedroom. Soon, she was washed, dressed, and ready, except for a few finishing touches. She brushed her blue hair until it glowed as stunningly as the clear sky over Trollzopolis. Then, she snapped on her amber spell bead bracelet and admired its golden color against her sky-blue sweater. A pair of sapphire and amber earrings completed her outfit. Sapphire just had time to gloss her lips before the hall clock chimed eight times. "I'm coming, I'm coming," she muttered to herself as she headed for the front door.

When she stepped outside, she could see her friends approaching from down the road. They made a bright and colorful group that was hard to miss. The sun gleamed like lightning in Topaz Trollhopper's golden hair. Ruby Trollman's enormous red hairdo towered over her friends like a fiery column. In contrast, Amethyst Van Der Troll's more subdued hairstyle bobbed like a cloud of pink cotton candy as she walked with her friends. When Sapphire's gaze finally landed on Onyx Von Trollenberg, she gave a little laugh. If her other three friends formed a fluffy rainbow of colorful hair and outfits, Onyx was the exact opposite. Onyx didn't go for complicated styles — or multiple colors. Today, as usual, her curly dark purple hair blew in the breeze above an all-black outfit accessorized with lots of spiky-looking black jewelry.

As Sapphire stood marveling at her very different friends, something weird began to happen. Far behind her friends, Sapphire saw a dark cloud. It was heading straight for them and moving very quickly. Sapphire waved her hands frantically to get her friends' attention. Onyx looked up and Sapphire pointed into the distance. "Look behind you!" she called, trying to make her soft voice carry far enough so they could hear her.

Sapphire squinted into the wind that had sprung up. The dark cloud looked like a mini tornado, or maybe some kind of dust devil, and it was inky-black and sort of solid-looking. It was such a beautiful day — where had this black cloud come from? As Sapphire looked on, horrified, it caught up to her friends. She watched as it seemed to twirl around them, making them cough and wave their arms.

"Ew! Get it OFF!" she heard one of them cry. It sounded like Ruby.

And then, just as quickly as it had appeared, the

3

thick cloud whirled off. Once it had left them, the BFFL ran, panting, and collapsed on Sapphire's front steps.

"What *was* that?" Amethyst coughed.

"I don't know," Sapphire admitted. "But look!" Inky-black scuff marks dotted the roadway, evidence of places where the tornado had touched down.

"It smelled nasty, too," Onyx said grimly.

"Ick!" Ruby screeched, looking in her ever-present hand mirror. "Look what it's done to my hair!" Sure enough, a gob of sticky black stuff smeared one side of Ruby's stratospheric 'do. "Frizz me out!" Ruby trilled dramatically. "I can't go to school looking like this!"

"Wow," Topaz gasped. "That is one big hunk of gunk in your hair, Ruby!"

Sapphire gave an inward sigh. Topaz meant well, but sometimes she was a little spacey. The last thing Ruby needed right now was someone pointing out how gross the gunk was.

"I know!" Amethyst piped up. "I'll spell it out." She fumbled with one of the amber spell beads on her bracelet and chanted:

**"From A to Z and one to ten,
Make Ruby's hair all fine again!"**

There was a small popping sound as the gob of goo

in Ruby's hair seemed to quiver for a second, but the spell had no effect. In fact, instead of disappearing, the gob became even more entwined in Ruby's hair. The trollz looked at one another in confusion. Spells might not always work the way the person casting the spell intended, but they always *worked*. And a clean-up spell was a pretty simple one that usually didn't require much spell power.

"That's funny," Topaz said.

"It is NOT funny!" Ruby said between gritted teeth.

"Oh, Ruby, I didn't mean it that way," Topaz assured her friend.

"You never do," Ruby hissed. There was nothing like a hairdo malfunction to give Ruby a major attack of the frizzies. It seemed that everything the BFFL said or did was just making her more upset.

"Come on, Ruby, it's not that bad," Onyx said soothingly.

"Oh sure, you think anything that's black is just great," Ruby shot back. "But to each her own, and I'd rather be bald than have anyone see me looking like this!"

"Sapphire, don't you have something that might

help?" Amethyst asked. The most diplomatic of the five, Amethyst was uncomfortable with confrontation. She preferred to keep things on an even keel at all times.

Sapphire checked her watch. She hated to be late, but usually they arrived at school with plenty of time to spare. Anyway, Sapphire's friends were worth a lot more than a few minutes to her. She'd do almost anything for any one of them. She looked thoughtful for a moment. "You know, I just might," she finally said. "Come on inside."

2

Better Living Through Chemistry

The girls ducked into Sapphire's house and headed into her bedroom.

"Way to go, troll," Amethyst said admiringly as she saw Sapphire's neatly arranged chemistry table in one corner of the room. "I knew you wouldn't let us down. If you don't have something that will get that goo off, no one will."

Sapphire was the amateur scientist of the group. A logical thinker, she loved the precision of such subjects as chemistry and math. She had set up a small but sophisticated laboratory in her bedroom where she performed experiments and sometimes even made her own lip gloss, nail polish, and other important cosmetics. "I just need to figure out what kind of stuff it is," she said modestly while Ruby fumed at the mirror.

"Ruby, sit over here," Sapphire suggested, pointing to a chair. "Just try to relax. This won't hurt a bit," she promised her friend as she gently tweezed a small amount of the gunk out of Ruby's hair. Sapphire sat down and examined the specimen under her microscope. "It looks oily," she announced. "Onyx, you said the tornado smelled nasty. What exactly did it smell like?"

Onyx pondered and said, "Kind of like skoot exhaust, but much stronger." Skoots were extremely popular motorized hover scooters that almost every troll over the age of ten used to get around. The girls rode them just about everywhere. It was only recently that they'd stopped using them to get to school because Ruby had begun creating super-tall hairdos that wouldn't fit comfortably under her helmet. And there was no *way* Ruby was going to let anything get in the way of a new hairdo.

As Amethyst had also sensibly pointed out, a little exercise once in awhile wasn't a bad thing, either. Even so, it was a definite fact that the BFFL — along with every other troll in Trollzopolis — probably spent more time on their skoots than off them.

"Hmmmm," Sapphire murmured as she began using a dropper to test different potions on the sticky goo. "Skoot exhaust is carbon-based. Maybe this is, too."

"What*EVER*," Ruby said testily. "Just. Get. It. Out. Of. My. Hair. OK?"

"Ruby, you forgot the magic word," Topaz innocently reminded her. Ruby shot her a withering look.

Topaz quickly backpedaled. "I mean, well, of course you're upset, Ruby," she stuttered. "I know you *meant* to say please like you normally do." This was pretty much a complete fib, since Ruby was famous for her princess attitude and the fact that she usually *didn't* say please. Or thank you. But right now, the friends were all trying to defuse a tense situation.

Amethyst hastily agreed with Topaz. "That's right."

"I think I've got it!" Sapphire announced. Everyone crowded around as she soaked a cotton ball with a clear liquid and began dabbing at Ruby's hair. Soon, the goo was gone. Ruby looked in the mirror and sniffed as she began primping, fluffing, and re-combing the section where the gunk had been. Finally, when her hair looked perfect again, Ruby turned to Sapphire with a disarming smile and said, "Thanks, Saph."

Then the BFFL all chimed in, too, with lavish praise for Sapphire's speedy solution to Ruby's hair crisis. Even laid-back Onyx gave Sapphire a wide grin as she said, "Nice going, Saph."

"Oh, you're welcome," Sapphire murmured, a little flustered by all the attention. "Really, it was nothing."

Then she looked at her watch again and gave a little yelp. "We've got to go right now," she urged her friends. They grabbed their stuff and hurried off to school. If the BFFL noticed that Sapphire was unusually quiet on the way, they didn't say anything. She was still very puzzled — and a little worried — over the way Amethyst's spell had seemed to bounce right off the gunk. *What was that all about?* she wondered. When spells didn't work, it meant there was a problem somewhere. But what was the problem? Sapphire was determined to figure out what was going on.

3

Trouble in Trollzopolis

That morning in science class, Sapphire raised her hand.

"Yes, Sapphire?" Mr. Trollheimer called.

"Mr. Trollheimer," Sapphire asked. "Is there a property that might affect a spell?"

"What do you mean?" Mr. Trollheimer wanted to know. "Many things can affect spells, but I'd need more information to give you a more specific answer."

"Well," Sapphire said slowly. "What if you tried to spell something to go away and it didn't? Are there substances that can make a spell kind of bounce off something? Or even backfire a little?"

"I see what you're getting at, Sapphire," Mr. Trollheimer replied, nodding. "If a substance is unusually resistant to magic, you might need a stronger spell to affect it. Or you might need to get more than one troll to pool their spell power. Or you might even need more amber spell beads. It all depends. Do you understand what I mean?"

"Yes," Sapphire said. "Thanks, Mr. Trollheimer." Cautiously, she exchanged glances with her friends. Onyx raised her eyebrows and Amethyst nodded thoughtfully. Ruby just fluffed her hair with one hand. She didn't really care what that gunky stuff was, as long as it was out of her hair. Topaz was looking out the window and Sapphire couldn't catch her eye.

In the front of the room, Mr. Trollheimer watched and said nothing. As usual, he knew more than he ever let on.

Later, in the lunchroom, Sapphire huddled with the BFFL crew. So far, they'd heard from two other trollz at school who'd seen the same weird tornadoes that morning, and now they were very curious. Sapphire was beyond curious. She was determined to get to the bottom of the whole thing.

"We need more information," Sapphire told her friends urgently.

"Well, if it's info you want, then we'd better head to

Fizzy's after school," Ruby added. Fizzy's Amber Caves Café was one of their favorite hangouts.

Onyx rolled her eyes. "Oh, you're just hoping Rock will be there as usual, so you can gush over his big muscles," she said. Rock Trollhammer was a hunky troll with biceps that unfortunately often seemed to be much larger than his brain. As far as Ruby was concerned, that just made him easier to twirl around her little finger.

"So what if I am?" Ruby said airily. "It's also the place to hear everything that's going on, so let's spell two birds with one bead, OK?"

"Ruby's right," Amethyst admitted. "If there's anything to find out, we'll hear about it there."

"Yeah," said Topaz excitedly. "And I can enjoy a trollburger while we're doing it."

"Well, I'm so glad we've all managed to convince ourselves that a trip to Fizzy's is really an educational adventure," said Onyx with heavy irony — irony that was lost on Ruby and Topaz, who were busy pumping their fists in the air.

"So we'll all meet at Fizzy's right after school, OK?" Amethyst reminded her friends.

"Yes!" said Topaz brightly.

"You got it, trollipop," added Ruby.

"Uh-huh," Sapphire murmured absently as she checked her watch. She did not want to be late getting to their first class after lunch.

"Whatever," Onyx muttered under her breath.

After school, the girls raced home to get their skoots, then headed straight to Fizzy's. Fizzy's Amber Caves Café was owned and operated by Fizzy himself, the crankiest troll ever to set foot in Trollzopolis. It was a constant mystery to the trollz how he managed to stay so crabby when he spent nearly all his time in the dim and relaxing environment of the café. Its amber walls perpetually glowed with a soft, inviting light, which was more than anyone would ever say about Fizzy himself. For someone who made a living in the hospitality industry, he was the complete opposite of welcoming.

It was never, "Hi, how can I help you?" or "What can I get you?" Instead, he usually greeted his customers with an ill-tempered blast of grouchy pronouncements.

"You kids better order something," Fizzy barked at the girls as they sauntered in. "Tables ain't free, ya know!"

"Of course we will, Fizzy," Ruby sang as the girls rolled their eyes at one another. Ruby was the self-appointed charmer of the group, and she made it her job to keep Fizzy out of his maximum cranky range. Her sugary sweet manners with him usually worked, too. Not that he was ever nice, but he was a little less nasty, which was better than nothing.

As the girls were sliding into their seats, a loud twang announced Flint Trollentino's entrance. Flint was a moody poet and self-styled emo rocker. He claimed that the vibe at Fizzy's was good for his music, and he wrote most of his songs there, much to Fizzy's dismay.

Now, as Flint strummed his ever-present guitar and began to wail his latest composition, Fizzy threw up his hands and rudely slammed the kitchen door so he wouldn't have to listen. Oblivious, Flint didn't miss a beat as he sang,

"I don't know what it is
But it's got me in a frizz

This pollution on top of us
Spells the end of Trollzopolis
This sticky cloud of misery
Won't let us just be
It's whirling into our lives
It's giving me the hives
It's a crying shame
Don't know who to blame
Run, run while you can
It's too late to try to make a stand!"

Of the five BFFL, Onyx was the most sympathetic to Flint. Like Flint, she herself was a little bit of a square peg, unusual and different from most other trollz. She could relate to Flint's determined pursuit of alternatives to the mainstream, and to the way he always marched — and sang and twanged — to a beat even she didn't always understand. She nodded coolly when Flint finished, which was actually high praise from the low-key Onyx.

Topaz was not only the most musically inclined of the girls, but she was also as open and enthusiastic as Onyx was dry and sarcastic. Now Topaz fixed Flint with her biggest smile. "Oh, Flint," she gushed. "That was wonderful!"

Flint tried to look modest. "Yeah, well, like, *someone* needs to speak up," he told her earnestly. "I'm just trying to keep our cool Trollzopolis deal from breaking up, know what I mean?" He grabbed his notebook. "Speak up, break up," he muttered as he scribbled with his black felt-tip pen.

"No," Sapphire suddenly spoke up. "I don't know what you mean, Flint."

"Well, like, did you not just listen to what I was singing?" Flint asked incredulously. "These tornadoes of doom are just taking over our fair city. It's like a sign that the party's over, and we need to do something about it before it's too late."

"But in your song you said it already *was* too late," Onyx pointed out reasonably.

"Yeah, but that's, like, poetic license, Onyx," Flint said with a hurt air. "The whole point of the song is that people need to wake UP," he continued. Then he snapped open his notebook again. "Break up, wake up," he mouthed as he scribbled furiously.

"Flint, what do you know about the tornadoes?" Sapphire asked him urgently.

"He knows I got a major sideswipe by one this morning on my way to school," a deep voice broke in.

It was Rock, entering Fizzy's with the rest of the posse: the adorable but shy Coal Trollwell, street-smart Jasper Trollhound, and rich whiz kid Alabaster Trollington III.

"You did?" Ruby gushed. "So did I!" She'd hated it at the time, but now the idea that the tornado goo gave her something in common with Rock was growing on her.

Rock sank into the chair next to her. "How'd you get it off?" he wanted to know.

"Well," Ruby began, "it was the most awful thing. It landed in my *hair*, right *here*," she went on, turning her head to show Rock more of her elaborate coif.

"Cool 'do," Rock commented, which only made Ruby preen even more.

"Why, thank you, Rock," she chimed, batting her eyelashes. If Ruby heard Onyx sigh heavily at her theatrics, she took no notice. Poor Rock was putty in Ruby's hands. Now he stared at her, completely rapt, as she spun the story of her close encounter with the gunk tornado. Soon, they were heavily involved in a one-on-one conversation while the rest of the group chattered on around them.

"What's with these crazy tornadoes, anyway?" Jasper exclaimed. "I can't have my posse getting slimed with gunk every time we're outside."

Coal nodded and smiled faintly. He wasn't known for being very talkative.

"They're turning up more and more all over," Alabaster put in. "They seem to come out of nowhere and spin away fast. No one's even trying to figure out what they are."

"Maybe it's time that changed," Sapphire said thoughtfully. Above all things, Sapphire was logical. For the rest of their time at Fizzy's, she turned the tornado problem over and over again in her head, trying to look at it from all angles so she could figure out a way to approach it.

"You're awfully quiet, Sapphire," Flint ventured after their food orders had come and gone and Sapphire still hadn't spoken.

"Mmmm," she answered absently. "I'm thinking. I wonder. . . ." With that, she stood up abruptly. "I've got to go," she announced. "See you all later!"

"What's up with her?" Jasper asked as Sapphire hurried out of Fizzy's.

"Beats me," Amethyst said.

"No idea," Topaz added with a shrug.

"If I know Sapphire — and I do — she's got an idea she wants to test out," Onyx said. "I wonder what it is."

4
Reaping the Whirlwind

Onyx had been right. Sapphire did have a plan. Quickly, she skooted home and grabbed a portable science kit her parents had given her the previous year for her birthday. Then she headed out into Trollzopolis. It was time to get to work.

She skooted from place to place. Wherever she stopped, her plan was the same. The science kit was filled with several small, sterile bottles for storing specimens. Patiently, Sapphire waited at each stop, vial in hand. Soon enough, she'd spy the telltale dark cloud. Then she'd race to where it was heading and try to collect a small sample of the tarry smoke residue. From the center of town to the edge of the woods, she did this with decidedly mixed feelings in a number of locations. The fact that she was able to spot so many tornadoes was great for her specimen collection, but it was very depressing to see how common the smelly swirls had become all over Trollzopolis.

Gasping and choking, Sapphire bravely stuck to her mission. Before long, she had filled every single specimen bottle. With a heavy heart, she skooted home so she could begin her work. She had about an hour before dinner to experiment, and she hoped that would be enough. After all, she still had homework to do, too.

First, she pulled down a few basic chemistry books from the shelf in her bedroom and looked up a few elements. Then she set up her lab. She already had a pretty good hunch that the stuff was carbon-based because the carbon dissolver she'd used on Ruby's hair had worked perfectly that morning. But exactly what kind of carbon was it? And where had it come from?

First, she examined a few different specimens under her microscope. They were definitely all the same. Close-up, she could see individual strands of the shiny, dense material that seemed to make up the tornado. The dark, sticky substance looked a bit like tar. She began testing the samples to see how they'd react to different substances. Finally, it was time to test her hunch.

She headed outside and started her skoot. She wasn't taking it for a ride, though. Instead, she held a clean, empty specimen bottle near the exhaust vent. When she'd managed to capture a tiny puff of skoot smoke, Sapphire sealed the bottle, turned off the skoot, and went back inside.

Twenty minutes later, Sapphire had her answer. This was really bad news. She fired up her computer and sent a group t-mail to the BFFL. Next, she grabbed her spell phone and dialed into the Chatter Line. By pressing a special sequence of buttons, Sapphire was able to set up a five-way conversation. She knew it wouldn't be long before her friends dialed in. Then she'd tell them the awful thing she'd discovered.

5

Sour on Skoots

"Sapphire, are you absolutely sure about this?" Amethyst wanted to know as soon as she got on the Chatter Line.

"I am completely certain," Sapphire assured her. "I tested and re-tested. The results are definite. Skoots run on a combination of magic and the old-fashioned internal combustion engine, which is powered by fossil fuels. So even though a skoot doesn't produce a lot of pollution on its own, each skoot does produce some.

Back in the day, when hardly anyone used skoots, the little exhaust puffs were naturally neutralized in the environment after a few days. But now, with so many people using skoots, and with the population of Trollzopolis steadily growing, it's just too much. The natural elements in the environment that normally absorb skoot exhaust just can't keep up."

"So the exhaust is coming together in the air to form these concentrated pollution tornadoes," Onyx summarized when she clicked into the conversation. By now, all five girls were on the line.

"But what does that mean?" Topaz wanted to know. "Do we have to give up our skoots?"

"Redial!" Ruby exclaimed incredulously. "Give up skoots?"

"Don't get in a frizzy," Sapphire tried to reassure her friends. "Listen, why don't we get together at my house and see if we can figure out a solution, OK? I'd like to show you my research." The girls agreed to meet in an hour. Much to Ruby's dismay, they also agreed to walk to Sapphire's house instead of using their skoots.

"I already walked today," she pointed out. "To school and back, remember? I mean, how much exercise does a girl need?"

"If you're not part of the solution, you're part of the problem," Onyx reminded her. "Wake up and smell the swamp gas, Ruby."

"Walk around and smell the pollution tornadoes is more like it," Ruby grumbled before hanging up. But she did agree. She didn't like it, but she'd do it, especially if it would help save Trollzopolis.

* * ✳ *

Later, at Sapphire's house, the girls pondered how to handle Sapphire's conclusion about the skoot pollution. They knew something had to be done soon, or all of Trollzopolis would suffer.

"What if the tornadoes just keep getting bigger and bigger?" Topaz asked anxiously, finally putting into words what they'd all been worrying about.

"It will be an environmental disaster," Sapphire said solemnly. "It will certainly be the end of beautiful Trollzopolis as we know it."

"We've got to figure out a way to solve this problem," Ruby said. "But it seems as if all we've been doing tonight is banging our heads against a wall." Her friends reluctantly agreed. They were no closer to an answer than they'd been earlier. The situation looked hopeless.

"I never thought I'd come to dread the sight of something black," Onyx mused, as she looked at the assortment of specimen bottles and slides on Sapphire's lab table. Idly, she began fingering one of her dangly earrings. Their carved facets sparkled in the light from Sapphire's desk lamp. Sapphire noticed the earrings and suddenly had an idea.

"What are your earrings made of, Onyx?" she asked.

"Ebonite, from the ancient ebonthorn pits," Onyx told her. "Why?"

"Just curious," Sapphire replied. It was too soon to tell anyone about the idea she had just had about how she might solve the pollution problem. What if she turned out to be wrong? After her friends had gone home, Sapphire took down a heavy book of trollz elements and looked up ebonite.

"*Ebonite is made from fossilized ebonthorn trees,*" she read. "*It is also a form of compressed carbon. As the tree dies and the dead wood ages, its molecules break down, growing denser and denser with each passing year. The substance that remains is hard, shiny ebonite.* Hmmm, I wonder."

She hurried through her homework. Once she had finished, she carefully laid out a new set of experiments on her lab table. When she finally got into bed that night, it was much later than usual. Tired as she was, Sapphire was still smiling as she pulled up her turquoise blue quilt and snuggled into her bed. She could hardly wait to see her friends the next morning and tell them about her plan. *Wait 'til they find out*, she thought sleepily as she drowsed off. *I have the solution.*

6

Sapphire Saves the Day

The next morning, Sapphire was up bright and early. Long before her alarm clock usually went off, she had been out to collect several new skoots-pollution tornado samples. Then she'd set up her final experiment.

"Eureka!" she cried as she realized everything had gone exactly as she'd planned.

By the time her friends arrived to pick her up for school, she was waiting in front of her house. With one hand in her pocket, she lounged nonchalantly against the door frame. In her other hand, she bounced a few small items that made a soft clicking sound as they tumbled against one another.

"Hey, Sapphire," Amethyst called out. "You're ready ahead of time today. I could see you standing there from way down the road."

"Well," Sapphire said, trying hard to be modest. "It's not every day I solve a pollution problem."

"Get out!" Ruby shouted. "You did it?"

"Wait," Onyx interrupted. "What are those dazzling gems?" Onyx, as usual, was riveted by anything black and shiny.

"Oh, these?" Now Sapphire tried to act casual. "These are the solution," she informed her friend as she tipped her arm over Onyx's outstretched palm and let the sparkling black gems tumble into her hand. The girls smiled knowingly at one another as they watched Onyx struggle to maintain her usual unflappable demeanor. Ultimately, cool won out, as usual, but still Onyx couldn't suppress a small gasp.

"They're gorgeous!" she breathed.

"Are they ebonite?" Topaz wanted to know.

"Uh-uh," Sapphire said, shaking her head.

"Then what are they?" Ruby demanded.

"They're concentrated skoot pollution," Sapphire informed them proudly.

Onyx jerked back, nearly spilling her handful of black gems. "What?" she wailed. "You mean I'm holding poison in my hand?"

"No, no," Sapphire hastened to console her. "They're completely neutralized. They're harmless," she clarified.

"You are the bomb, troll," Ruby put in admiringly. "Only you could figure out a way to take icky pollution and turn it into something beautiful."

"Well, once I figured out the chemical chain, it was really very easy," Sapphire said. "It was just a question of finding the right amount of compression to change the soft pollution residue into a hardened substance. In fact, all we need to do is to get everyone to use a simple plastic bag filter and one of these." She held up a small plastic device that looked a little bit like a hair iron. "First, riders place the filter over the exhaust vent. Then, after they use their skoot, they just squeeze the contents of the filter bag into this press. I call it the converter, because it converts the pollution into these pellets."

"How do they squeeze smoke?" Topaz wanted to know.

"Oh, it only looks like smoke when it's puffing out from the skoot's exhaust vent," Sapphire explained. "Smoke is actually made up of tiny particles. Once it's collected in the bag filter, the particles join together to form strands. After a person's been riding around on a skoot for awhile, the stuff in the filter bag will start to look more like the stuff that gunked Ruby's hair," she went on. "Try it. You'll see."

"Where'd you get the converter?" Amethyst inquired.

"I made it out of some stuff that was lying around the house," Sapphire admitted. "Its base is a plant press. I just fiddled around with it to get rid of the openings that let the juice out. This way it's more of a compressor."

Plant presses were used to extract juices from a variety of plants that grew in Trollzopolis. Edible plants were juiced to flavor foods. Other plants were juiced to make dyes and other useful compounds. Most troll households had at least one plant press.

Onyx still cradled the shiny black pellets in her hands. "They're completely harmless, right?" Onyx asked. Sapphire nodded.

"So, can I make jewelry with some of them?" Onyx asked.

Amethyst snorted. "Who'd want jewelry made out of concentrated pollution?" she wanted to know.

"Smell the swamp gas, troll," Ruby informed

her, with a meaningful glance at Onyx. "Who do ya think?"

"Anyway, it's not *really* concentrated pollution," Sapphire told them. "It's simply hardened carbon — similar to ebonite, or even diamonds," she pointed out. "Onyx, feel free to use as many as you want, but believe me, once we get everyone in Trollzopolis on board with the skoots pollution solution, there will be way too many of these for anyone to manage to recycle all of them."

"So what will you do with them?" Topaz asked, a perplexed furrow creasing her brow.

"Well, the carbon stones are a somewhat natural substance," Sapphire assured her. "And I have been thinking about that, and doing a little reconnaissance."

"Reconna-what?" Topaz asked.

"Reconnaissance," Sapphire repeated. "You know, just looking around at places that might be good for storing the carbon stones. Really, only the Haunted Woods is big enough to absorb all of them. I was thinking the pond at the edge might be a good spot."

"Pond? I don't remember a pond," Topaz mused.

"Oh, Tope," Ruby scoffed. "You never remember *anything*!"

"Hey, we've gotta go," Sapphire reminded everyone, looking at her watch. They headed off to school, anxious to tell everyone about Sapphire's discovery, and about her pollution solution.

7

Putting the Plan Into Action

In science class, Sapphire explained her idea to Mr. Trollheimer. She showed him the pollution converter along with some of the pellets she'd made. He was impressed by her ingenuity, and even offered to give her extra credit if she wrote up her research and experiments.

"What are you going to do with all the pellets once more and more people begin using your invention?" he inquired.

"Well, they're very hard and kind of pretty," Sapphire began, "so we thought we'd try to make jewelry out of them." This was true, even if it wasn't the whole truth. When it came right down to it, Sapphire suddenly felt reluctant to tell Mr. Trollheimer about the pond she'd discovered. In the first place, the Haunted Woods was sort of off-limits, and not exactly a place trollz were supposed to go. Although the pond was at the edge of it,

Sapphire really didn't want to admit to even being near the woods to Mr. Trollheimer. After all, why go there?

"Interesting idea," was all he said, and to Sapphire's relief he didn't ask any further questions.

After school, the BFFL headed to Fizzy's. The collection bag filters attached to their skoots attracted a lot of attention, and once the girls spread the word that the filters would put an end to the gunk tornadoes, they had tons of orders for the filters and converters.

They were in business! The idea was that everyone who used the converter would turn the tiny stones over to Sapphire once a week. Since the pellets were so small, this was easily a job one troll could handle. On collection day, Sapphire would put them all together in a large wagon that she attached to her skoot. Then she'd head for the pond and dump them in. Simple.

The first few weeks of Sapphire's pollution solution went perfectly. Even with the enormous use of skoots in Trollzopolis, the tiny pellets never amounted to more than a small handful from each troll. Meanwhile, the air grew cleaner day by day and soon the smog tornadoes had disappeared entirely.

But a few weeks later, something terrible happened. . . . Something worse than the original tornado problem.

8

Oops! I Polluted Again

Sapphire was just heading out to the edge of the Haunted Woods when it began to rain lightly. She thought about turning back, but decided to keep going. So far, the rain only amounted to a drop or two here and there, and Sapphire was nearly there. She'd just move fast and zip back home as quickly as possible. Then, as she wheeled up to the edge of the woods, it began to rain a little harder.

Sapphire wished she'd brought a raincoat, for she was already starting to get soaked. Still, a job was a job. She shook the rain off her hair and reached into the wagon to grab a handful of the pellets. Instead of hard little beads, though, her hand hit something slimy. "Yuck!" she exclaimed as she yanked her hand back.

Sapphire looked at her hand in disbelief. Inky-black goo dripped from her fingers. Dreading what she would see, she peered into the wagon more carefully. Incredibly, the pellets seemed to be melting in the rain.

The rain began pouring down even harder. This was a disaster! Sapphire thought about venturing to the edge of the pond to look in and see what was going on with the pellets she'd dropped in there during the previous weeks. The rain got the better of her, though. She decided to skoot quickly back home. At least that way she could keep the pellets in her wagon from adding to the problem.

As soon as she got home, she braved the pouring rain to wheel the pellet wagon into the backyard shed. She hoped that by keeping them relatively dry in the shed, the pellets would stop deteriorating. *Maybe they'll even harden again,* she thought, though the scientist in her knew that was unlikely.

By the time she got inside, she was completely drenched. And there was even more bad news inside.

"Sapphire, is that you?" her mother called from the kitchen. "Come look at this!"

Sapphire made her way back toward the kitchen. What she saw when she got there took her breath away. Her mother stood at the sink, her hands covered in the same kind of black gunk that had been on Sapphire's hands after she'd touched the melting pellets.

"What in Trollzopolis is going on? When I turned on the water it looked gray coming out of the tap, and it smelled terrible. Then strands of sticky black stuff started coming out, too," Mrs. Trollzawa explained. "I tried spelling them away, but they only got worse." Then she caught sight of Sapphire's equally black-smeared hand. "Sapphire, do *you* know what this is?"

"I have a pretty good idea," Sapphire confessed. "Mom, I think I've made a terrible mistake, and I've gotta go fix it right now!" She started to head for her room, then stopped and turned back to her mom. "Mom, just for now, please don't use the water, OK?" Sapphire begged. Her mother started to say something, but Sapphire cut her off. "Mom, this is my problem and I've got to fix it," she insisted.

"Just be careful, whatever you do," she heard her mom call after her as she raced to call her friends. *If only I'd been more careful to begin with,* Sapphire thought to herself. *Then all of Trollzopolis wouldn't be in trouble right now!*

9

Saph's Pollution Solution

As she'd requested, Sapphire's friends met her at the edge of the Haunted Woods. The rain had cleared up, although it was still damp and muddy underfoot. She was relieved to see they'd all followed her urgent instructions and were wearing rubber gloves and carrying large, heavy-duty trash bags. Cautiously, they ventured to the edge of the pond. What they saw made them gasp.

The once crystalline pond water was now thick and muddy-looking. Thin, black tendrils swirled up from the bottom. As each tendril hit the surface of the water, an oily sheen began to spread.

"It's not just that it's causing more pollution," Sapphire quickly informed her friends. "The fact that it's begun to penetrate the groundwater means that even the Amber Caves are threatened!"

"No!" Onyx cried. If the Amber Caves were destroyed, the magic that kept Trollzopolis running would disappear with them. There would be no spells, no color, and no beauty. Everything would turn gray and lifeless.

The Amber Caves were a vast underground complex of natural caverns formed by a continuous stream of dripping liquid amber. In the ancient days, the gush of free-flowing amber combined with underground streams to carve the caverns out of the bedrock below Trollzopolis. When the ancient gush had slowed, the amber began dripping slowly from the caverns' lofty ceilings, forming the mighty columns of stalactites and stalagmites that gave the Amber Caves their awe-inspiring architecture. At its center was the place of ultimate trollz magic power, the stump of the original tree where the amber still flowed.

This amber that still trickled among the glowing amber halls and rooms created the magic that powered much of Trollzopolis and the trollz way of life. There were small streams of amber here and there in Trollzopolis, but the amber in the caves was special. The Amber Caves were where girl trollz were taken as babies to get a few drops of amber placed in their belly buttons in a secret ceremony. Later, when they were a little older, this amber gave each troll her own special magic. Any threat to the Amber Caves was nothing short of a disaster.

"I should have realized this sooner," Sapphire blamed herself. "The way Am's spell seemed to bounce off the pollution gunk was a sign of two important things. First, we were dealing with an especially strong substance. Second, the skoot pollution was already affecting the entire Trollzopolis environment, including its magic. Unfortunately, my so-called solution only sped up the process."

"Wait a minute," Amethyst said. "Remember when you asked Mr. Trollheimer about how to get around stuff that was resistant to spells?"

"Ye-es," Sapphire said slowly. "I think I see where you're going, but you know, my mom tried to spell the stuff in the sink, too. And just like your spell with Ruby's hair, it only made things worse."

"But Mr. Trollheimer said that pooling magic might provide better results," Onyx reminded them.

"Let's try it," Ruby put in. "Anything is better than having to reach into this disgusting pond. What do we have to lose?"

"That's what I'm worried about," Sapphire admitted. "Who knows what will happen if we try a spell and it doesn't work?"

"It can't hurt," Onyx reasoned. "Come on, Saph, let's at least give it a try."

The girls took off their gloves — they didn't want anything interrupting the flow of power between them. Then they joined hands and stood in a circle around the pond. Sapphire squeezed her eyes shut as she thought furiously for a moment. When she opened them she began to speak in a strong, clear voice:

**"True friends joined to make things right,
Turn this pond's water clear and bright!"**

Then each girl tossed a bead from her amber spell bead bracelet into the pond. The beads plinked in and the pond began to ripple. The girls held their breath, hoping their spell would work. Suddenly, a large, greasy bubble began to rise from the center of the pond.

"Well, something's happening," Ruby whispered.

"*Shhhh,*" Sapphire hissed.

The bubble grew larger and larger, and its oily sheen reflected the light in a shimmering rainbow. The rainbow would have been pretty if it hadn't been attached to a huge, ugly gray bubble. Then with an unbelievably loud and reverberating burping sound, the bubble burst, sending a foul smell into the air. The pond seemed a little darker and murkier than before.

10

Dirty Work

"Now what can we do?" Topaz wailed.

"If spelling won't work, we have to start somewhere else," Sapphire informed everyone grimly. "And the first thing to do is to recover as many pellets as we can."

"Then let's get to work," Amethyst said bravely, pulling on her gloves.

It was hard work retrieving the pellets. Each girl took up a position at the edge of the pond and then stretched her arm all the way down into the cloudy water and carefully scooped out as many pellets as she could. The rubber gloves kept the gunk from smearing onto their hands, but the gloves couldn't protect their entire arms. It was cold, wet, and smelly work.

Still, they kept at it until each had a bulging trash bag full of slimy, deteriorating stones. Finally, it looked as if they'd recovered almost all of them. They felt around as much of the pond as they could and peered into its murky depths.

Sapphire surveyed the bulky garbage bags. "This looks to be about the same amount I remember dumping in," she said. "Do you think we really might have all of them?"

Just then, the small pond began churning as if it were a mighty ocean. Its tiny ripples swelled into choppy waves as greasy bubbles hissed and popped on its surface. A gurgling voice seemed to be laughing in a sinister way. The girls watched in horror as the black strands of pollution began swirling violently inside the pond. As they swirled, they began to merge with one another, twisting into a heavy coil of solid matter.

Now, something seemed to be emerging from within the pond. Sapphire recognized the malevolent eyes of the evil gremlin, Simon. The girls jumped back with a gasp as Simon burst from the pond in an enormous gush of dirty, smelly water. Sapphire's heart sank even farther when she realized what he had gripped in one hand: the end of the thick black rope the swirling pollution strands had formed. As he whipped it out of the pond, it began collapsing onto itself, shrinking in a tornado spiral that finally ended in Simon's outstretched palm as a black, shiny lump — the biggest ball of concentrated pollution Sapphire had ever seen.

"No, my little trollkins," Simon crooned, hovering in the air above the pond's roiling surface. "I don't think you have all of them, after all."

11

The Battle For Trollzopolis

"So it was you who caused the pollution!" Sapphire accused Simon.

"No." Simon shook his head, flinging drops of dirty water into their eyes. "The pollution was something you trollz created all on your own. Let's just say I knew how to take advantage of it. Thanks for the opportunity," he sneered.

Simon was every troll's worst creepy nightmare. A twisted gremlin trapped in the body of an innocent-looking small boy, the girls forever regretted the awful mistake they'd made when they had accidentally freed Simon from his 3,000-year "nap" in the Shadow World. They'd been tricked, first by Simon's nasty sidekick, the ogre-dog Snarf. Somehow he'd managed to persuade the girls that he was really a woman named Miss

Tourmaline, who could help them when their gems were beginning to dim.

Locked in "Miss Tourmaline's" shop, the girls had unwittingly fled straight into the Shadow World, a creepy place of ghostly shadows. That's where they'd found Simon, who'd fooled them by pretending to be a lost little boy. Thinking they were rescuing a child who'd accidentally fallen into the horrible, howling Shadow World, they'd taken him back with them through the portal to Trollzopolis. That's when they'd realized the truth about Simon. He wasn't a little boy at all but, rather, a wicked gremlin bent on revenge and cruelty. They'd managed to defeat him that time, but now that he'd been freed from his Shadow World prison, he was always trying to trick his way back into Trollzopolis. He was desperate to avenge himself by destroying Trollzopolis and enslaving the trollz who lived there.

"I knew I hadn't seen that pond before," Topaz mused.

"*You* put it here?" Sapphire gasped, flashing her eyes at Simon.

"I knew a little busybody like you wouldn't be able to resist it," Simon gloated.

Sapphire was crushed. *How could I have been so stupid?* she berated herself. She'd fallen right into Simon's wicked trap, and now Trollzopolis was doomed.

"Don't be too hard on yourself," Simon mocked Sapphire, using his considerable powers to read what was going through her mind. "The pollution would have wrecked Trollzopolis sooner or later. I just didn't want to wait that long! Why wait when I can wreck it NOW!" he howled gleefully. Then he rose up threateningly, slowly spinning above the pond. He began thrusting the black rock toward each of the girls.

As Simon whirled, bringing the black rock closer first to one girl and then another, Onyx came to a sickening realization: The rock had a powerful aura of its own. As Simon moved it around, beams of blinding black light shot from its surface, temporarily blinding her. Worse, each time the rock came near her, she felt it sapping more and more of her magic. She already felt weak and dizzy from the sunspots flashing before her eyes. Soon she — and her friends — would be completely in Simon's power.

Simon continued to turn lazily in the air. He acted as if he had all the time in the world. Onyx knew that if she couldn't manage to break free and fight back, Simon would get his way for sure. As Simon passed the rock by Onyx a third time — this time so close it nearly touched her face — Onyx steeled herself to take a chance. Simon had just moved past her, and soon he'd have his back to her. It was now or never.

Her own body seemed to fight her as she struggled against the paralyzing effects of the rock. It was a major effort to direct one hand to grab hold of the amber spell bead bracelet with its dangling ebonthorn charm circling her other wrist. She only hoped her plan might work. In a quavering voice, Onyx spelled:

**"Stone of black as deep as night,
Help us win this desperate fight!"**

There was a cracking sound and a flash of light. Simon quivered and seemed to slip a little, one foot splashing down into the pond. His furious roar reverberated through the woods. Onyx still felt weak and low on magic, but she hoped that if she managed to shake Simon's hold on her and her friends a little bit, they would be able to exploit it.

Ruby's ears were still ringing from Simon's deafening roar when she heard an answering sound. Only one creature could make that kind of horrible, hollering cross between a bark and a snarl. It was Snarf, Simon's half-ogre, half-pit bull henchdog. Snarf's magic never rose higher than half-power, but sometimes this, combined with his deadly intentions and amazing stupidity, seemed only to make him more dangerous.

He bounded into the clearing, and Ruby gritted her teeth. If Onyx had managed to fight back against Simon and the terrible magic of the black rock, then maybe she could, too. Then, there was a blast of red light as Snarf launched an explosive spell in her direction.

12
Smoke and Mirrors

Ruby gave an ear-piercing scream when Snarf's spell hit her. Then it was Simon's turn to shriek.

"You idiot! You fool!" he bellowed to Snarf. With a flash of choking orange smoke, Snarf yelped in agony and disappeared.

Ruby had managed to work her trusty hand mirror out of her pocket and used it to bounce Snarf's spell away from herself and onto Simon. Between Onyx's spell and Ruby's quick thinking, Simon's power had been considerably weakened. The girls all felt their own powers flickering back to life. Amid the pandemonium and howling around them, the BFFL took heart.

Unfortunately, Simon seemed to sense their recovery before they were able to put anything into effect.

"It's not over yet," he warned them. "As long as I hold THIS!" With that, he clutched the black rock more tightly. With a horrible sinking feeling, the girls watched as the stone began to throb and glow.

"Such a pretty little stone," he taunted them. "A stone of DOOM!"

Sapphire knew that Simon was right. As long as one of the stones remained, it still spelled trouble for Trollzopolis. And because this stone was far larger than any of the others, its deadly evil was that many times more powerful. How could they fight back?

"Don't be stupid," Onyx called in a voice far braver than she actually felt. "You're making a big mistake, Simon."

"How *dare* you speak to me that way!" Simon fumed. All his attention was focused on Onyx now. Menacingly, he stepped out of the pond and headed for Onyx. "I'll make you pay for your insolence," he threatened.

"Go on," Onyx said scornfully. "I dare you, Simon."

Simon was nearly upon her. When he heard this last remark, he swelled to nearly twice his size. His eyes flashed and his mouth opened wide, revealing his ugly pointed teeth. "Try this on for size," he bellowed, making a fist as if to throw the deadly stone straight at her. But Onyx beat him to it.

She whipped off her black necklace and hurled it with amazing speed directly into Simon's gaping mouth. He made a dreadful gurgling sound and clutched his throat to no avail. Onyx's aim had been perfect, and Simon had no choice but to swallow the necklace that had lodged itself deep in his throat.

A terrifying black cloud began pouring out of Simon's mouth, swirling around him to form an enormous tornado. Its howling winds tore at the girls' hair and clothing. The tornado continued to swirl faster and faster. Soon Simon was engulfed within its whirling column.

The tornado continued to speed up, but now it seemed to be shrinking. With an earsplitting shriek, it vanished into the pond, taking Simon with it. When the smoke cleared, the girls saw that the pond had disappeared as completely as if it had never been there. All that remained was the shiny black rock. They stared at it, mesmerized, until a sound made them look in Onyx's direction.

She swayed on her feet, moaning in pain. Her eyelids fluttered and her knees buckled beneath her. She was fainting from the strain of her struggle with Simon.

"Help me!" Topaz cried to her friends as she grabbed Onyx's arm, trying to break her fall.

13

Filling In the Puzzle

Several hours later, the girls had managed to get Onyx — and all the remaining pollution pellets, including the large one left behind by Simon — to the Von Trollenberg home. Now Onyx was resting in her room while the girls tried to figure out what had happened.

"I just kept getting weaker and weaker," Amethyst confessed.

"Me, too," Topaz chimed in.

"But then Onyx managed to break Simon's hold a little," Sapphire said wonderingly. "How did she do that?"

Ruby spoke up. "She mentioned a black stone in her spell," she reminded them. "But I don't think she was talking about the pollution stones. Because they were working for Simon, right?"

Onyx nodded weakly from her bed. "I used the

ebonthorn on my amber spell bead bracelet," she croaked. "My special stone . . . and it's black, too."

"Hush now, child, you need your rest." Obsidian surprised everyone as she bustled into the room. Obsidian was wise beyond reckoning in troll lore, and she ran the Spell Shack at the mall. The girls had always found her to be amazingly helpful — especially when it came to untangling Simon's twisted plots to take over Trollzopolis.

"Obsidian!" the girls cried in unison. "What are you doing here?"

"Ah," Obsidian intoned. "Well, Onyx, your mother is worried about you. She called over to the Spell Shack and told me you'd been up to something that had shocked your system, and asked me to look in. I've had a pretty good idea of what Simon's been up to, so I wasted no time once I got her call," Obsidian assured them. "Let's have a look at you." She strode briskly over to Onyx's bedside.

Onyx meekly submitted to Obsidian's examination. "Hmmm," Obsidian sniffed as she shone a small pen-light into Onyx's startled eyes. "Well, no harm done, I suppose."

"Obsidian," Sapphire ventured timidly. "I've been thinking."

"About time for that," Obsidian observed tartly.

Sapphire looked so crestfallen that even Obsidian relented. "Don't blame yourself, Sapphire," she said softly, placing a warm and reassuring hand on Sapphire's shoulder. "You were tricked by a master of deception. Simon has had 3,000 years to plot his revenge — hardly a fair match for a young girl like you," she pointed out. "And yet . . ." she mused. "You girls did it. I'm so proud of you."

"But how?" Amethyst wanted to know. "What really happened to Simon back there?"

"Onyx was smart to remember her ebonthorn," Obsidian explained. "Because it, too, is a dense, black stone, it was able to fight the power of Simon's pollution stone fire for fire, as it were. But the ebonthorn proved to be the stronger stone because it comes from nature, whereas the pollution stone was based only on concentrated filth."

"What about at the end, when Onyx hurled her necklace into Simon's mouth?" Topaz wanted to know. "What happened then?"

"Well, I guess that was no ordinary necklace,"

Obsidian went on, smiling broadly. Propped on her pillows, Onyx nodded weakly.

"Our Onyx has always been very fond of the color black," Obsidian continued. "Perhaps some of the stones in her necklace were not ordinary jet or even ebonthorn," she suggested. "Maybe she had added some of the pollution stones to her necklace, too?"

"That's right," Amethyst exclaimed. "I remember that!"

"And, of course, once she'd worn them for awhile, they would have begun to absorb Onyx's own natural powers," Obsidian elaborated. "So they proved especially potent against such slime as Simon. When he was forced to swallow the same substances he was trying to wield against Trollzopolis, it began eating away at him from the inside."

"Will it kill him?" Topaz wanted to know.

"No, it won't," Obsidian replied. "But it will take him some time to recover from that kind of blow. Our Onyx showed great bravery, which is always a potent weapon against someone like Simon."

Onyx's smile may have been a pale shadow of itself, but the sparkle in her eyes practically lit up the room as

Obsidian spoke. Then Onyx pointed to the mirror over her dresser and raised her eyebrows. Her friends looked puzzled, but Obsidian nodded knowingly.

"Ah, yes," Obsidian agreed. "Ruby really distinguished herself there."

"What are you talking about?" Topaz wanted to know.

"When Ruby made Snarf's spell backfire!" Amethyst recalled. "How did she do that?"

"Perhaps Ruby will explain that herself," Obsidian said, smiling.

Ruby blushed until her face matched her flaming hair. This was extremely unusual behavior for Ruby, who usually put the chill in cool. "I, uh, used my pocket mirror," she confided hesitantly. "It reflected Snarf's spell onto Simon."

"Ruby, that was so smart!" Amethyst exclaimed.

"Well, I've always said a girl's best friend is her mirror," Ruby said teasingly, back to her old self again. Then she turned to Onyx with a big grin. "And, of course, her jewelry, too!"

At Ruby's lighthearted mention of jewelry, Sapphire's expression darkened. She was the only one of the BFFL who'd left once they'd gotten Onyx settled at home.

She'd rushed back to her own house, returning as she'd promised within a half hour. Now, she seemed troubled by what she'd just heard.

"But what about these?" she asked slowly. Then she reached into a pocket and pulled out a handful of glittering golden gems.

"Oh, Sapphire," cried Topaz, reaching out her hand. "They're gorgeous! What are they?"

Sapphire pulled her hand away so Topaz couldn't touch them. Topaz looked puzzled, and then hurt, as her eyes sought Obsidian.

"Don't worry, Sapphire, those are harmless now," Obsidian assured her.

"You mean those are pollution stones?" Topaz gasped.

Sapphire nodded. She felt so terrible. However unwittingly, it had been her pollution solution that had given Simon another portal into Trollzopolis. Her mind had been racing furiously throughout the ordeal in the Haunted Woods and in spite of everything, she had had to try out one more theory. When she'd gone home, she'd hurriedly fiddled around with her chemistry set.

Sapphire knew from all her previous experiments how to extract the essence of certain roots and stems.

Once she'd even succeeded in creating her own blumeria perfume by using this technique to distill flowers. She had an idea that maybe she could create a solution that might really neutralize the pellets. She started with some ebonthorn leaves, reasoning that the concentrated amounts of carbon in ebonthorn were more likely to form a bond with the carbon-based pollution.

Sapphire had counted on the powerful ebonthorn facet to overpower the pollution. If that happened, its carbon would become further concentrated and anything unhealthy in it would be completely neutralized. First, she put the leaves into a plant press. Then, she quickly boiled the resulting liquid over her Bunsen burner. It wasn't long before she'd distilled a clear liquid with the consistency of honey.

She had used a dropper to add her ebonthorn solution to some of the leftover pellets. Then she'd compressed them a second time. The result was a sparkling golden gem that looked a bit like a diamond. These were the stones that Topaz was so anxious to get a better look at right now. Sapphire planned to convert all the remaining pellets this way to make them all completely harmless.

"I only wish I'd thought of neutralizing them sooner," Sapphire said glumly.

"Oh, Sapphire, you can't blame yourself for what happened," Amethyst consoled her. "Simon is always looking for a way to get his powers back."

"Yeah, but I gave it to him," Sapphire insisted. "I thought I'd come up with such a great idea, but I hadn't really thought it through. If I'd just tested everything more carefully, I would have realized that the stones could start deteriorating in water. Anyway, changing the pollution into something else just postpones the problem. I can neutralize the remaining stones, but that doesn't really solve the bigger problem of skoot exhaust polluting the air of Trollzopolis."

"Think it through this time. Go back to the beginning and think it through," Obsidian advised. "I'm sure you'll find the answer, Sapphire. I have great confidence in you. And now let's leave Onyx so she can rest." And with that, she hustled the girls out of Onyx's room, and back to their own homes.

14

Thinking It Through

"Think it through. Go back to the beginning," Sapphire muttered later that night as she pored over the encyclopedia. She was determined to solve the skoot pollution problem, and to do it right this time. But how?

She'd been working for hours, and yet she was no closer to a solution than she'd been at the start. It had been a long day and she was exhausted. Finally, it was just too late. Sapphire put her things away and fell into a troubled sleep.

She had a strange dream. She dreamed she was in a smoky cave, trying to find her way to the entrance. She could see a faint light, which she followed. The light grew brighter and brighter until Sapphire came out of the smoke into a glowing golden room. Its brightness blinded her at first, but when her eyes finally adjusted to the light, she saw that it came from glittering piles of golden stones. They looked similar to the pollution stones Sapphire had created, but different, too. They were a deeper shade of gold and seemed to glow from within, as if a tiny fire burned deep inside them.

"What are they?" Sapphire wondered to herself.

"They are what was in the beginning," a reedy little voice seemed to whisper in her ear. Sapphire looked around, startled. She'd been alone in her dream up until now, but as she looked around she spied an impossibly ancient troll.

"What do you mean?" Sapphire asked urgently. Somehow she knew that this was the answer to her problem. This ancient troll could help her.

"Go back to the beginning," the ancient troll intoned.

Still in her dream, Sapphire moved closer to the golden gems. She reached out to pick one up. When she touched it, it felt strangely warm. She gasped and woke up.

Sapphire had the answer at last. She hopped out of bed and began what she felt certain would be her final experiment on skoot pollution.

15

Forever Amber

An hour later, Sapphire hummed happily to herself as she arranged her hair into an elaborate braid. Usually, she stuck to fairly simple styles, but today was special. She couldn't wait to share her incredible news with the BFFL crew.

As they walked to school, she quickly outlined her idea.

"Are you sure it will work?" Onyx wanted to know.

Sapphire nodded confidently. "I checked and double-checked," she assured them. "I did exactly what Obsidian suggested. I went back to the beginning and then I thought it all the way through."

"It's so obvious when you think about it," Amethyst mused. "I can't believe no one thought of trying that before."

"Sometimes it's hardest to see what's right under your nose, I guess," Topaz said.

The girls stopped and stared at their friend. Topaz had an uncanny way of putting her finger on the heart of the matter. She was right, as usual. It was often hardest to see the thing that was right in front of you. As far as the skoots went, all of the trollz in Trollzopolis had made that mistake.

"To think that all along they could have been running on pure amber power," Ruby said, shaking her mile-high hairdo.

Skoots had always run on a combination of magic and a small regular engine that used a fossil fuel. The fossil fuels were used to get the motors started, but they also burned carbon. What Sapphire had figured out was a way to convert the skoot motors to ones that use liquid amber instead of fossil fuel. This way, the skoots ran on pure, non-toxic magic.

Better yet, once a tiny amount of Trollzopolis's plentiful liquid amber was placed in the engine, it was permanent. Not only were the skoots non-polluting, but they never needed refueling again. Best of all, ordinary amber worked fine, so there was no need to take special amber from the Amber Caves.

"I'm going to ask Mr. Trollheimer if he can help me work on the converters," Sapphire said. "Amber power is pure and clean. I want everyone to use its non-polluting power from now on."

"We'll all be able to keep our skoots," Amethyst added.

"And keep Trollzopolis beautiful," Topaz pointed out.

"And best of all," Ruby summed up, "once Sapphire gets her amber converters to every skoot-riding troll in Trollzopolis . . ."

"We'll never have to worry about pollution again!" they shouted.

Sapphire looked at her four Best Friends For Life and grinned. She wouldn't trade her friends, or her great life in Trollzopolis, for anything. And now, thanks to her terrific pollution solution, she wouldn't have to.

Sapphire suddenly remembered an old Trollzopolis saying her mom had taught her: "Into every life a little rain will fall." It meant that everyone experienced tough times and had to face things they couldn't control — and there was certainly nothing anyone could do about the weather. But in figuring out a way to get rid of the tornadoes, Sapphire had proven that another old Trollzopolis saying was also true: "Everyone can make a difference if they'll only try." Sapphire was glad she hadn't given up, and that she'd kept trying even though her first plan had been a disaster. By sticking to it and thinking things through, she'd made a permanent difference. Now, skoot pollution would never rear its ugly head again. Knowing that felt good, and it *was* good — for Sapphire, her friends, and every other troll in Trollzopolis.

Congratrollations!

You get 50 Trollars to spend on Trollz.com
just for buying this book! After you've read
the book go to Trollz.com and type in
the code below to collect your 50 Trollars
and have a chance to earn 300 more!

0-439-70003-5uz498di4751v

Create your own Trollz™ on TROLLZ.com

For more trollular fun check out
scholastic.com/trollz

You and your BFFL's (Best Friends For Life) **can**

- ☆ start your own Trollz™ Book Club
- ☆ print invites and bookmarks
- ☆ and get more cool stuff

Coming this Fall

Fun and fashion with a magical twist!

Available now
wherever toys
are sold!

Big Hair is Back!

Trollz™

It's A Hair Thing!™

Create Your Own Trollz™ Online
TROLLZ.com

Meet the Trollz — five best friends who share everything together, including their newfound magic powers! Hang out with the Trollz... they'll put a spell on you!